To McHarrell and Julia,
for uniting culture and Christmas
–G.E.T.

To Lorien, Maryn, and Kristin
for all your help
–G.F.

DAVID O. MCKAY
3 1404 00875 4316

By Garen Eileen Thomas • Illustrated by Guy Francis

Jump at the Sun

Hyperion Books for Children
New York

Text by Garen Eileen Thomas

For information address Hyperion Books for Children, 114 Fifth Avenue, New York, New York 10011-5690.

Printed in Mexico

First Edition
3 5 7 9 10 8 6 4 2

Reinforced binding

This book is set in Fink Condensed.

Library of Congress Cataloging-in-Publication Data on file.
ISBN 0-7868-5166-X

Visit www.hyperionbooksforchildren.com

'Twas the night before Christmas. The very last hour.
He was all out of breath and he needed to shower.

For
Santa

Wrapped gifts were now stacked where Yule wishes had lain.
'Twas time to return to the North Pole again.

Poor Santa lamented his potbellied girth,
Though he'd loved every cookie, for what that was worth,
He thought of his house, what awaited him there—
And how he'd trade in these boots for a comfortable pair.

So he loaded his sleigh up with empty cloth sacks.
Next, he gave his stout reindeer a pat on their backs,
And then up, up, up and away they all flew
Through the day and the night. Little Rudolph did, too.

Then off in the distance shone a sight for sore eyes:
His sweet humble home (disguising a surprise . . .).
Santa sauntered so softly through the open front door
And he pulled off his suit, which he left on the floor,

MERRY
CHRISTMAS

When who should appear but the light of his life—
The behind-the-scenes maven, his loving boss-wife—
Who held out his kente to resounding applause,
And shouted out with the elves,

Welcome Home, Santa Kwaz!

It was time to rejoice in the Santa Kwaz way—
To celebrate Kwanzaa this 26th day
Of December. And then, in a marvelous twist,

The elves approached Santa with their very own list:
"We've gifts for *you*, Santa," they said with great glee,
Which they fetched from their spots 'round the great Christmas tree.

First Nia, Kuumba, and Kuji-cha-gulia,
Then Imani, Umoja, Ujamaa, and Ujima
Placed each grand Kwanzaa item upon Santa's lap,
Which brought tears to his eyes, the jolly old sap.

And each night through the seventh, the family showed
Their deep pride in their roots as their cups overflowed.

Till the last eve was ending, and Santa decreed
He had *more* Kwanzaa spirit, and that he would need
His deer to go on one more of their night flights,
But they'd have to go higher, to reach greater heights.

So the elves and the missus packed themselves in the sleigh,
And when Santa was seated, they set out on their way

To the top of the trees, to the galaxy's end,
As he thought of the message he wanted to send.
Then using his magic, which he gets from above,
Santa lit up the heavens in colors of love.
'Twas the most glorious vision in the whole universe . . .

HAPPY KWANZA
PEACEFUL MEN

. . . Santa's hope and his blessing for the people of Earth.

You can celebrate Kwanzaa, just like the Kwazes!

Umoja's
pride unites the family

Kujichagulia
is determined always
to speak her mind

Ujima
is responsible for
solving problems

Ujamaa
cooperates and trades fairly

Nia's
purpose is to keep
the community great

Kuumba
is the most
creative of all

Imani's
faith and vision keep
all our dreams alive